For David and Gemma - GA

To Rita Greene with much affection - VC

ORCHARD BOOKS
96 Leonard Street, London EC2A 4XD
Orchard Books Australia
Unit 31/56 O'Riordan Street, Alexandria, NSW 2015
First published in Great Britain in 2002
ISBN 1 84121 693 3
Text © Purple Enterprises Ltd 2002
Illustrations © Vanessa Cabban 2002
The rights of Giles Andreae to be identified as the author and Vanessa Cabban
to be identified as the illustrator of this Work have been asserted by them
in accordance with the Copyright, Designs and Patents Act, 1988.
A CIP catalogue record for this book is available from the British Library
10 9 8 7 6 5 4 3 2 1
Printed in Hong Kong/China

Heaven's Having You

Giles Andreae

and

Vanessa Cabban

ORCHARD BOOKS

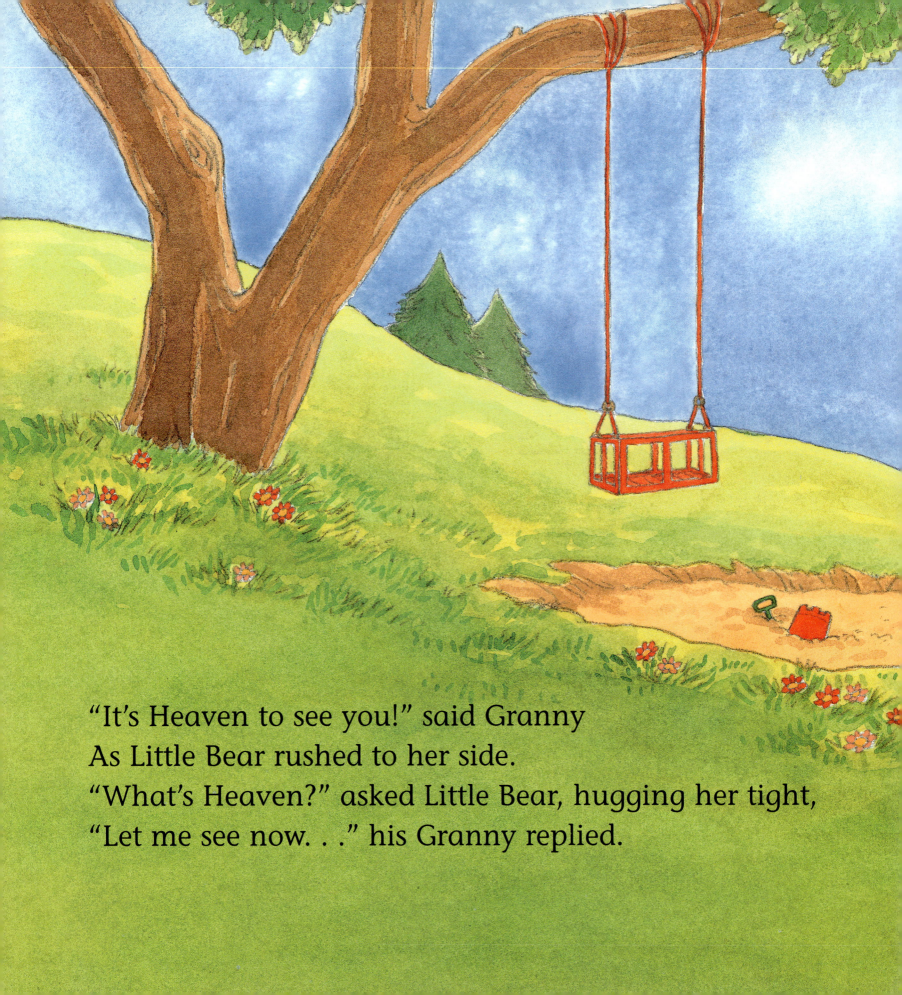

"It's Heaven to see you!" said Granny
As Little Bear rushed to her side.
"What's Heaven?" asked Little Bear, hugging her tight,
"Let me see now. . ." his Granny replied.

"It's not all that easy to tell you
Because Heaven is so many things,
Sometimes it's just seeing Grandpa Bear's face
As he's helping you play on the swings.

Sometimes it's something exciting

Like looking for monsters in dens,

But often it's just going walking together

Or watching you play with your friends.

It's feeding the ducks at the duckpond
And letting them eat from your hand,

It's seeing the wonderful shapes that you make
And the castles you build in the sand.

It's hearing the stories you tell us
And thinking you're ever so clever,
It's something we do that we made up ourselves
Like rubbing our noses together.

It's chasing you right round the garden

And hearing you shriek with delight,

It's lying flat out while you sit on my tummy

And jiggle with all of your might.

It's making your favourites at teatime
And eating them up in one go,
It's having our own little secrets to keep
And our own special places we know.

It's running a bath full of bubbles
And helping you clamber up in,

It's running a bath full of bubbles
And helping you clamber up in,

It's holding you tight in a huge fluffy towel

And it's even the smell of your skin.

It's wrapping you up
in a blanket
And feeling your warm rosy cheeks,

It's holding you tight in a huge fluffy towel

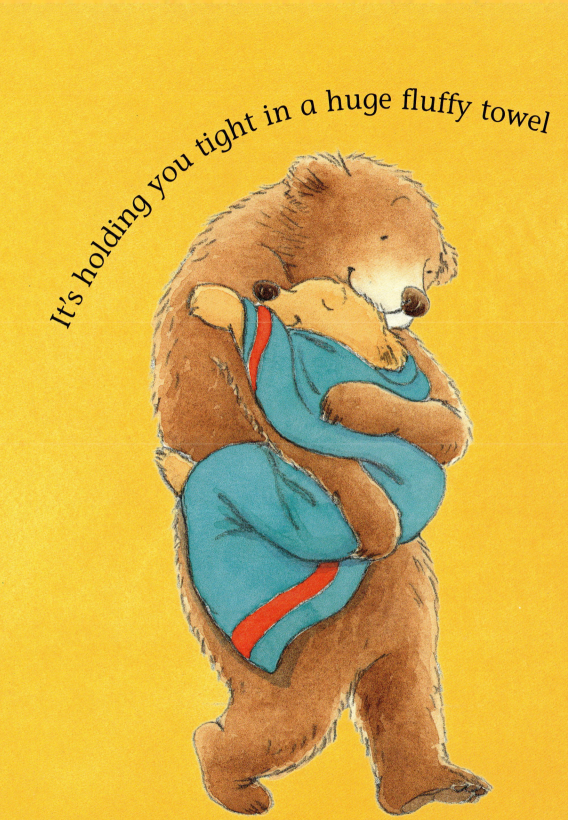

And it's even the smell of your skin.

It's wrapping you up
　　in a blanket
And feeling your warm rosy cheeks,

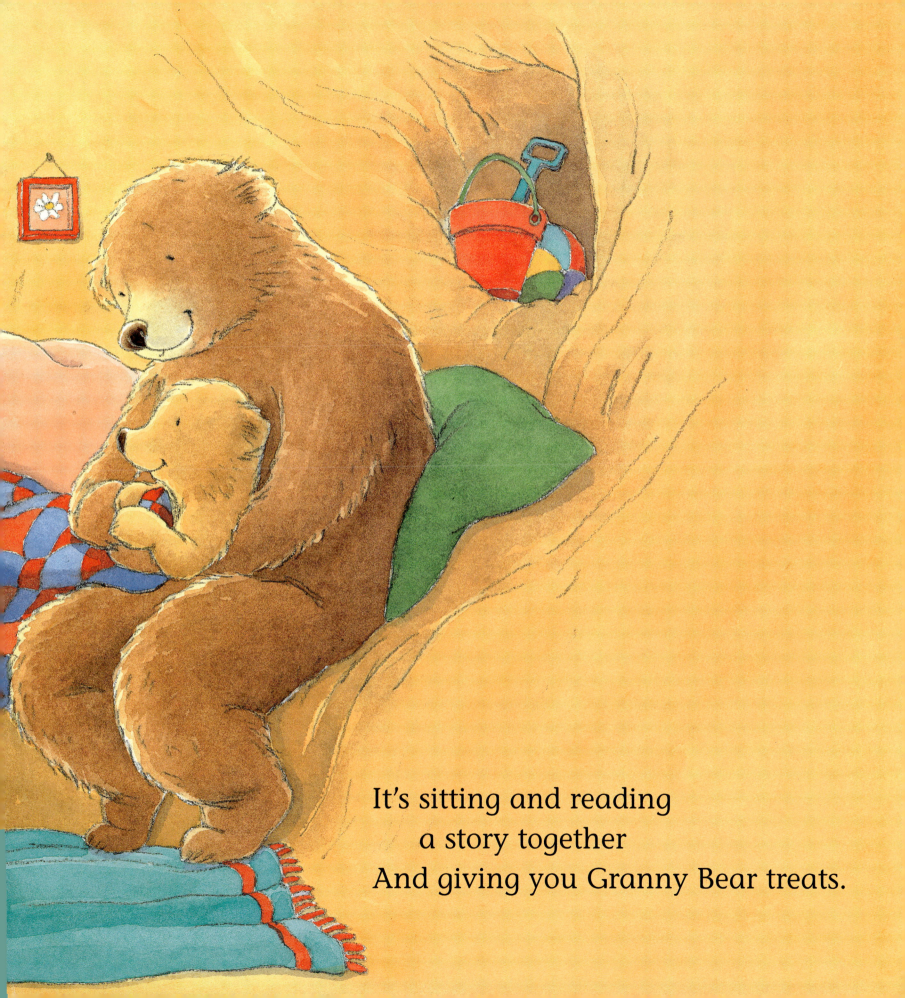

It's sitting and reading
a story together
And giving you Granny Bear treats.

And then when it comes round to home time
Heaven is kissing goodbye,

It's giving your Grandpa
a lovely big hug
And it's seeing
the pride in his eye.

Heaven is always around us
In so many things that we do,

But one thing is true above all, Little Bear –

Heaven is just having you."